A SNAKY ESCAPE!

"At six feet long and sixty pounds, this is our favorite slithery friend," Jumpin' Jack said. "Meet . . . Bubba the boa!"

Little Jim grabbed the end of the red sheet. With one tug he yanked it off, revealing the giant cage underneath it. From where they were sitting, all Frank and Joe could see was a few rocks and some sand. Jumpin' Jack stepped toward the cage and peered inside. He had a big frown on his face.

Little Jim looked horrified. "No . . . this can't be happening . . . ," he muttered.

Principal Green appeared at the edge of the stage. She'd been sitting in the front row. "What is it? What's wrong?" she asked.

Jumpin' Jack rubbed his forehead with his hands. Frank and Joe had never seen him so upset. "It's Bubba!" he said, his voice panicked. "He's gone!"

CATCH UP ON ALL THE HARDY BOYS® SECRET FILES

THE HARDY BOYS®

SECRET FILES #17

 The Great Escape

BY **FRANKLIN W. DIXON**

ILLUSTRATED BY **SCOTT BURROUGHS**

ALADDIN ▪ NEW YORK LONDON TORONTO SYDNEY NEW DELHI

ALADDIN

An imprint of Simon & Schuster Children's Publishing Division
1230 Avenue of the Americas, New York, NY 10020
First Aladdin paperback edition April 2015
Text copyright © 2015 by Simon & Schuster, Inc.
Illustrations copyright © 2015 by Scott Burroughs
All rights reserved, including the right of reproduction in whole or in part in any form.
ALADDIN is a trademark of Simon & Schuster, Inc., and related logo is a registered trademark of Simon & Schuster, Inc.
THE HARDY BOYS is a registered trademark of Simon & Schuster, Inc.
For information about special discounts for bulk purchases, please contact
Simon & Schuster Special Sales at 1-866-506-1949 or business@simonandschuster.com.
The Simon & Schuster Speakers Bureau can bring authors to your live event. For more information or to book an event contact the Simon & Schuster Speakers Bureau at
1-866-248-3049 or visit our website at www.simonspeakers.com.
Series design by Lisa Vega
Cover design by Karina Granda
The text of this book was set in Garamond.
Manufactured in the United States of America 0315 OFF
10 9 8 7 6 5 4 3 2 1
Library of Congress Control Number 2014957781
ISBN 978-1-4814-2267-3 (pbk)
ISBN 978-1-4814-2268-0 (eBook)

CONTENTS

The Great Escape

1

Welcome, Jumpin' Jack!

Did you hear that Channel Eleven News is going to be here tonight?" Frank Hardy, holding jungle scenery in both hands, squeezed through the back curtains of the stage in the Bayport Elementary auditorium. The giant wooden tree he was carrying was heavy. His whole face was red.

Luckily, his brother, Joe Hardy, was holding on to the other side of it, helping Frank set it down at

the back of the stage. Suddenly it looked as if they were lost in a forest. "It's the biggest news story this year!" Joe exclaimed. He pointed to a newspaper that was lying offstage. The headline read STARS OF THE HIT TELEVISION SHOW *CRAZY CRITTERS* COME TO BAYPORT ELEMENTARY!

Frank wiped the sweat from his forehead. "I wonder if Jumpin' Jack is as crazy in real life as he is on his show—"

"Of course he is!" Chet Morton called from the

front of the stage. He was kneeling down, painting a giant sign with Cissy Zermeño. The sign read THE KIDS OF BAYPORT ELEMENTARY WELCOME THE *CRAZY CRITTERS* GANG!

"I mean . . . who else would make all these special requests? He wanted his own personal massage chair in the dressing room," Cissy said, and laughed. She sat up, tucking her feet beneath her as she continued to paint. She was wearing neon green high-tops, the laces bright white.

Cissy was talking about the list of things Jack and Jim had requested for their show at Bayport Elementary. Jack's assistant had sent the list to Principal Green. Jack wanted special snacks for backstage, a massage chair to sit in before and after the show, and green towels to clean up with in case of accidents. (Green was his favorite color.) Frank and Joe's good friend Phil Cohen was helping put everything together. Even though Frank knew that all the requests were a bit silly, that didn't change the way he thought of Jumpin' Jack.

Jumpin' Jack and his sidekick, Little Jim, had been on television for years, starring in their own show. Frank and Joe had spent hours watching Jumpin' Jack and Little Jim tame tigers and bears. Jumpin' Jack had jumped on top of alligators. He'd held giant pythons around his neck and climbed trees in South America. Sometimes it seemed like there was nothing he couldn't do. Now he was coming to Bayport Elementary with all kinds of wild animals. The show was going to raise money for their school. Frank and Joe had thought someone was playing a joke on them when they'd first heard the news. It had just seemed too good to be true.

Just then Principal Green came through the back doors of the auditorium. She stared at the stage, past the currently empty seats, which would be full later. She scanned the wooden trees and vines Frank and Joe had set up. She watched Cissy and Chet painting signs. Then she walked by a few other kids who were working with the auditorium's sound system. They'd all stayed after school to help get ready for the big event.

"This looks great. Keep up the good work!" she called out, her voice booming down the aisle. "Jumpin' Jack and Little Jim will be pulling up at seven o'clock, and the show starts at seven thirty. We have less than two hours to finish!"

Cissy started painting a little faster. "We still have three more signs to make," she said. "Did you hear that more than four hundred people are coming tonight?"

"Yeah," Joe said. "Principal Green said the show sold out in less than an hour. All the tickets—gone! Just like that!"

While Joe and Cissy talked, Frank moved the last piece of scenery into place. The small wooden flowers looked so real, they could've sprouted out of the stage. "What do you think?" he asked.

Chet jumped down from the stage and ran up the aisle, not turning around until he was almost twenty rows back. "It's awesome!" he yelled. "Looks like a jungle, right here in Bayport."

Joe looked up at the towering trees. The Bayport High School Art Department had made each leaf look so real. Every branch was painted with five different shades of brown. There were colorful exotic flowers. At the back of the stage the high school students had painted a giant mural of a sunset, with a winding river beneath it. If Joe squinted a little bit, it was easy to imagine he was somewhere else. It was just like the places Jack and Jim visited on their show.

As Joe scanned the stage, looking for anything that was off, he heard the shriek and hiss of a speaker. It was coming from somewhere behind the curtain. "We should go see if Phil needs any help," he said to Frank, knowing their friend was working on the "tech room," where all of the special sound equipment was. He waved his older brother behind the curtain.

Backstage was dark, with only one light above them. Joe stepped around boxes and different set pieces from the recent school play, *Cinderella*. There was a giant pumpkin cart and a fake staircase that led nowhere. They crept toward the noise. A

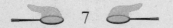

speaker screeched again. The sound was so loud that Joe had to cover his ears.

When they turned into the hallway behind the back curtain, they saw that one of the tech room doors was open. Their friend Phil Cohen was inside, standing with a bunch of wires in his hand. He turned the knobs on the speakers, but they only screeched more loudly.

"We just have to fix this. Then we're done," Mr. Rodriguez, the technology teacher, said. He kneeled down and kept unplugging and plugging cords into the speakers.

"This is incredible, Phil," Frank said, walking over to a long table covered in snacks. His hand hovered over a bowl of chocolates. "Can I take one?"

"Actually . . . those were a special request," Phil said. He pulled a list from his pocket and showed it to the boys. "Chocolate bonbons, gummy bears—

green only—sparkling lemonade, and lemon drops. Jumpin' Jack's assistant asked for them. See? It's all right here."

Meanwhile Joe sat down on Jumpin' Jack's massage chair. He flipped a switch, and it rumbled and shook. "OoooOOOhhhh-KaaaaaAAAAAy. We woooon't eaaaaat anythiiiiing," he said, his voice changing from the chair's vibration.

Beside him one of the dressing tables was stacked with green towels. The room looked completely different from how it normally looked during school plays. Phil had even hung up framed posters from *Crazy Critters*.

Mr. Rodriguez went behind one of the speakers and turned a knob on the back of it, plugging a cord into the outlet. "Finally!" he said as the room filled with classical music. "We got it to work!"

"I guess I'm done here . . . ," Phil said. "What else is left to do?"

"Cissy and Chet are finishing signs, and then we have to put up streamers on the driveway outside. Principal Green said Jumpin' Jack and Little Jim will be here in less than two hours," Frank said.

"Then what are we waiting for?" Phil asked. He grabbed the remote from the massage chair and shut the chair off. Joe finally stopped shaking. "Let's go finish up. We can do the streamers inside, and then we can try to have a perfect view when their *Crazy Critter* van pulls up outside."

"Great idea!" Frank said as he headed for the door. Joe and Phil followed close behind. "I can't wait. This is going to be the biggest night in Bayport history!"

2

The Big Night

"Places, everyone! Hold those signs up so they can see!" Principal Green called as the neon green van pulled up the driveway of Bayport Elementary. A huge crowd of kids stood outside. Parents were in rows behind them, cheering and clapping. There were also a few protesters, holding signs. Some people didn't like the fact that the animals were used in the show.

"Can you see anything?" Frank asked. He moved his head back and forth, but Chet was right in front of him. Chet's sign blocked part of Frank's view.

"Just the front of the van," Chet said as he looked around the bend. "I can't see who's driving. There are too many people in the way." The sidewalk across the street was packed. Kids stood on the fence holding signs that said WELCOME, JUMPIN' JACK! and WE LOVE CRAZY CRITTERS!

Then the van pulled up the long driveway and stopped right in front of the school's main entrance. Now that it was closer, Frank and Joe could see the giant vines and leaves painted on its sides. There were tiny painted monkeys and birds hidden in them.

A news reporter with huge, bright blond hair stood right outside the school's front doors. Her cameraman stood beside her. The light on his camera was so bright, it lit up the entire crowd. "Jumpin' Jack has just arrived at Bayport Elementary, where hundreds of kids and their parents have shown up for this crazy night," she said into her microphone. "The money raised from ticket sales will all go to the Bayport Elementary Activities Fund. It helps keep Bayport's air and water clean, and our streets clear of litter."

Joe stood on his tippy toes, trying to see inside the van. Little Jim was in the driver's seat—Joe could tell by his hair. Little Jim was shorter than Jack, and his thick white hair always stuck up in a hundred different directions. Frank had seen pictures of Albert Einstein, and thought Little Jim looked a lot like him.

Joe tried to peek over Chet and Phil's shoulders to get a glimpse of Jumpin' Jack. As he inched closer, Jumpin' Jack stepped out of the passenger side of the van. He was wearing the famous green jumpsuit and tall brown boots he always wore on the show. "Why, howdy-howdy-hey, Bayport Elementary!" he yelled to the crowd.

Frank and Joe clapped as loudly as they could.

Chet jumped up and down, waving his sign. All around them, kids were yelling and cheering. A little boy sat on his dad's shoulders, waving his stuffed monkey in the air.

"I'm so happy to be here tonight to help raise money for your school," Jumpin' Jack yelled. "Little Jim and I have been touring the country for our new book, *Crazy Camels*, the follow-up to *Crazy Toads* and *Crazy Monkeys*. In just two days we'll be in New York City, then on to Boston and Maine."

As Jumpin' Jack spoke to the crowd, Little Jim opened the back of the van and brought a few cages out. They were all covered with black fabric. "Those must be the animals," Frank whispered to Joe. "I wonder which ones he brought."

Little Jim put the cages on a rolling cart, then moved the cart inside. Jumpin' Jack wasn't far behind him. He greeted Principal Green and the news reporter, then followed Jim in. When he was gone, Principal Green finally turned to the giant crowd. "The auditorium will open in just ten minutes!" she yelled. "Have your tickets ready to give to the attendant at the door."

"I wish we got to go in early," Chet said, turning to his friends. "You'd think after all that work we did, they'd at least give us front-row seats."

Phil laughed. "I know, but I'd sit in the very last row if those were the only seats they had. I can't believe we actually get to see Jumpin' Jack and Little Jim's show live. Right here at our school!"

The crowd started lining up outside the front doors. Frank, Joe, and their friends moved toward the entrance, pulling their tickets from their pockets. People dropped their signs into a pile on the sidewalk.

"Do you think they brought Trixie the monkey?" a blond girl beside them asked her friend.

"I wanna see Bubba," a girl with freckles answered.

"Which one is he?" the blond girl asked.

Which one is Bubba? Frank knew he shouldn't eavesdrop, but it was hard to just listen to that

 17

question. Bubba was his favorite animal out of all the ones Jumpin' Jack had on the show. "Bubba is Jumpin' Jack's boa constrictor," Frank said loudly. "He's ginormous! He's one of the stars of the show . . . like the third host!"

The girls nodded, then continued talking about Trixie the monkey. Within minutes the doors opened and the crowd broke into cheers.

"It's time!" Joe said. He smiled, his blue eyes wide. Frank hadn't seen him this happy since the Bandits had gotten into the baseball championships.

"Let's go," Frank said, grabbing his little brother's arm and pulling him toward the door. "I can't wait for the show to start!"

The auditorium was dark. A spotlight was on the closed curtains on the stage, making a giant white circle. The audience was still whispering. A few first graders next to Frank and Joe were scared that

Jumpin' Jack and Little Jim might have brought tarantulas.

Then Jumpin' Jack stepped through the curtain, and the crowd clapped and cheered. A giant owl was perched on Jack's arm, which was covered with a heavy glove. The bird stared out at the audience with its big black eyes. "Howdy-howdy-hey, Bayport Elementary!" Jumpin' Jack yelled again, and everyone just cheered more loudly. "We have a fantastic show for you tonight. This is my good friend Kipp, a great horned owl. What do you think, Kipp? Should we start the show?"

The owl just looked out at the audience. It barely moved at all.

"In owl language that means, 'Yes! Let's do this!' So without further ado . . ."

The whole audience took a deep breath, getting ready to say Jumpin' Jack's famous opening words. "Welcome to our world of Crazy Critters!"

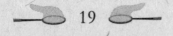

The curtains pulled back, revealing the jungle scenery Frank and Joe had helped put together. It looked even better from the audience. The stage crew had hung green garland across the stage, and Little Jim stood underneath the fake vines. He had a giant bird perched on his arm too—a hawk. The hawk was almost all brown, with reddish feathers on his head and tail.

"Meet our friend Thomas!" Little Jim called out. "He's a red-tailed hawk, which can be found in most of the United States, from Alaska to as far south as Panama. He's a bird of prey, and his kind is often called a 'chicken hawk,' though they don't like that. You'd never eat a chicken, would you, Thomas?"

The bird turned its head, which made it look like it said no. Frank was almost twenty seats back, but he could've sworn he saw Jim pop a treat into the bird's mouth to make him do that.

"We're going to need a very special volunteer

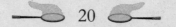

20

to come up here and meet Thomas and Kipp. Who thinks they'd like to hold one of these birds of prey?" Jumpin' Jack asked.

A hundred hands shot up into the air. "Mee, meeee!" one of the first graders next to Frank cried. Jumpin' Jack went down the stage stairs, started up the aisle, and finally stopped next to their row.

"You!" Jumpin' Jack finally said, pointing to Joe, whose hand was in the air. "Come up onstage and meet Kipp and Thomas. Come on, now!" he repeated, grabbing Joe's arm as he led him up the aisle.

Joe was smiling so much, his cheeks hurt. He'd only ever been onstage for the school talent show months before, and the whole week before he'd had butterflies in his stomach. Now he was going to be with Jumpin' Jack and Little Jim—two of his favorite people ever. He was so excited, his hands were shaking.

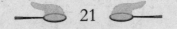

When they were finally onstage, Jumpin' Jack gave Joe a thick glove to put on his hand. He then placed Kipp on Joe's gloved hand. "What's your name?" Jumpin' Jack asked. "Kipp wants a proper introduction."

"Um . . . Joe," Joe said into the microphone.

"What do you think, Kipp? Do you like your new friend Joe?" The owl raised its head as if it were

saying yes. Then Little Jim came up from behind Joe and put the hawk on his arm. It was heavy. Joe tried to stand up straight and keep looking out at the audience so he wouldn't scare the giant birds.

"You're being very brave!" Jumpin' Jack said. "Let's have a round of applause for Joe and his two new friends!"

The whole audience clapped and cheered. Joe could see his friends in the crowd as Jumpin' Jack took the birds off his arm and Joe left the stage. Frank, Phil, Chet, and Cissy were standing up, cheering for him. "That was so cool!" Phil said when Joe finally reached his seat. "Weren't you scared?"

Joe admitted that he was, just a little. But he couldn't really tell them everything—the show was already moving on. Little Jim brought out a giant lizard named Rodrigo, and six different second graders went up onstage. The lizard was nearly five feet long, and it took all of them to hold it.

Next up was the tiny monkey, Trixie. Trixie did tricks. She could dance when Little Jim told her to. She did backflips and made funny yelling noises. At one point they called ten people onto the stage, adults and children. Trixie climbed all over them like they were trees.

The show had gone on for a bit longer when Jumpin' Jack turned to the audience with a grin. "Now for the star of our show, one of our most famous Crazy Critters."

Little Jim wheeled out a giant box with a red sheet over it. He put it in the center of the stage, where everyone could see. "Oh, man!" Frank whispered to his brother. "It's Bubba, right? It has to be."

"At six feet long and sixty pounds, this is one of our favorite slithery friends," Jumpin' Jack said. "Meet . . . Bubba the boa!"

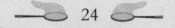 24

Little Jim grabbed the end of the red sheet. With one tug he yanked it off, revealing the giant cage underneath it. From where they were sitting, all Frank and Joe could see was a few rocks and some sand. Jumpin' Jack stepped toward the cage and peered inside. He had a big frown on his face.

Little Jim looked horrified. "No . . . this can't be happening . . . ," he muttered.

Principal Green appeared at the edge of the stage. She'd been sitting in the front row. "What is it? What's wrong?" she asked.

Jumpin' Jack rubbed his forehead with his hands. Frank and Joe had never seen him so upset. "It's Bubba!" he said, his voice panicked. "He's gone!"

3

Snake on the Loose!

The snake! The snake is missing!" an older woman behind Joe and Frank yelled. She jumped onto her seat, looking at the floor below. Other people jumped to their feet too, scared looks on their faces.

"How could they have lost the snake?" another man behind them asked.

The first graders beside Frank and Joe looked scared. A girl with blond pigtails started to cry. Frank and Joe slid out of their row and walked closer to the stage, trying to hear what Jumpin' Jack was saying. Principal Green had made her way up onto the stage and whispered something into Jumpin' Jack's ear.

"No . . . he was stolen!" Jumpin' Jack replied. "Someone took the top off the cage and stole him."

Principal Green grabbed the microphone. "Everyone, please remain calm," she said. "The snake is not missing. Someone took it out of its cage. It may have been put in a different cage or still be in Jumpin' Jack's van. Please leave the auditorium while we try to figure out what happened."

All the lights in the auditorium came on. People started leaving the auditorium and heading into the main lobby of the school. Little Jim and Jumpin' Jack hurried around the stage, looking at all the cages where they kept the animals. They checked the cages where they put the owl and hawk, and the one with the giant lizard. Bubba was nowhere to be found.

Frank, Joe, and their friends waited until most of the other people had left, then went up onstage to help. "Could they have left one of the cages in the dressing room?" Phil asked. "I can check if there's anything in there."

Jumpin' Jack's cheeks were bright red. He never got angry on the show, but Frank and Joe could tell he was about to start yelling. "He was just here before the show started. Right behind that curtain!" he yelled,

pointing offstage. "I saw him myself. And there was a lid on his cage. There's no way he could've gotten out. Someone took him! Someone took Bubba!"

"We'll find him," Principal Green said. "He must've been misplaced. Could he have been moved to a different cage?"

"Possibly," Little Jim said. "There was so much going on right before the show. Maybe someone backstage put him somewhere else. Or maybe he was in the wrong cage."

"Or maybe he was stolen!" Jumpin' Jack repeated. He kept rubbing his head with his hand. "Maybe one of your students took him when I wasn't looking!"

Principal Green frowned. "I don't think a Bayport student would do that, Jack. We'll get to the bottom of this. I promise."

"Do you think that could've happened?" Frank

whispered to Joe. "Who would want a giant boa constrictor?"

Joe shook his head. "I don't know. But if a student stole Bubba, it will be all over the news. They'll get in so much trouble."

Just then a group of parents and some kids came into the auditorium and walked right up to the stage. There were a few couples with young children, and a few men whom Joe recognized as dads of some of the third graders. "Principal Green!" one man in front said. "People outside want their money back for their tickets. The show lasted only a half hour, not even. What are you going to tell them? Can we come back inside or not?"

Principal Green looked like she might cry. "I don't see that there's any way the show can go on tonight," she said. "Maybe we can postpone it. How long are you staying in Bayport, Jack? Is there any way we can do the show tomorrow, once this all gets sorted out?"

"*If* this all gets sorted out!" Jumpin' Jack yelled. "If we can't find Bubba, the tickets won't be your only problem. That snake is worth thousands of dollars!"

"Please," Principal Green said. "I promise we'll find the snake. Can we just reschedule this show for tomorrow night? Will you stay one more day in Bayport?"

Jumpin' Jack glanced sideways at Little Jim. Jim just shrugged. "Fine," Jack said. "One more day, but only if you find Bubba. One of your students must have him somewhere. . . ."

"I'll go tell the crowd outside," Principal Green said. "Tomorrow night the show will go on, and Bubba will be there. We'll find him!"

As Principal Green walked out the door, the parents following behind her, Jumpin' Jack looked worried. "She says she'll find him," he mumbled, "but how?"

Cissy plopped down by the side of the stage.

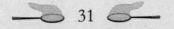

"If Bubba doesn't show up, we did all that work for nothing. Everyone will be so upset," she said. "What are we going to do?"

Frank and Joe looked at the empty cage. The metal lid was still on it, just like Jack and Jim had said. The two boys noticed the metal clips that held the lid in place, although they were flipped up now. "There's no way the snake could've gotten out of there on his own," Frank whispered.

"I know," Joe agreed. "Jack is right. Someone must've taken him. But who? And when?"

They had less than twenty-four hours to find the missing snake and return it to Jumpin' Jack. Had a Bayport student taken Bubba? Would they find the snake in time?

"Let's go," Frank said, nudging his brother toward the back of the stage, where the snake had last been seen. "We have a lot of work to do."

The Six Ws

Frank stumbled around backstage, nearly tripping over a small cage with two wild squirrels inside it. When he finally found the light, he turned it on. All of backstage came into view. Jumpin' Jack and Little Jim were there, standing over the empty tank they had moved after Bubba had gone missing. Cages were stacked beside the wall. Frank noticed a few of the animals from the beginning of the show—Kipp the owl and Thomas the hawk.

"What are you doing here?" Jumpin' Jack asked.

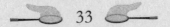

His face was still bright red, and his hair was a mess.

"We're here to help," Joe said. "We think we can find out who took Bubba. We just need to ask you a few questions."

Frank took out the notebook he always carried in his back pocket. Whenever he and his brother had a mystery they needed to solve, he was sure to write down every clue they found. They always started with the six *W*s: Who, What, When, Where, Why, and How. It reminded him of the giant jigsaw puzzles his grandparents used to get them for Christmas. Sometimes it took a while to put all the pieces together.

"Can you think of anyone who would want Bubba?" Frank asked. He wrote *WHO* at the top of the page and underlined it.

Little Jim kept shaking his head. "No idea."

"Maybe some kid who wanted a pet snake," Jumpin' Jack said. "It has to be a student here. Who else could it be?"

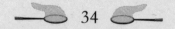

Frank wrote *Bayport student* underneath *WHO* and frowned. He hoped Jumpin' Jack wasn't right. Besides, how would a student have gotten backstage? How would they have carried the snake away?

"It could have been anyone who wanted the snake as a pet," Joe said. "Maybe it wasn't a student. There were some protesters outside too. It could have been one of them."

Frank wrote down, *someone who wanted Bubba as a pet*, under *Bayport student*, then *protesters*. He'd seen the small group outside. There had been about ten of them, and they didn't like that Jumpin' Jack kept his animals in cages when he was traveling on tour. They held signs that said FREE TRIXIE! and THOMAS DESERVES BETTER!

"We know the What. That part is easy," Joe said. "Bubba the boa constrictor. Well, he is green. He's about six feet long. He was right here before the show, right in this tank backstage."

35

Jumpin' Jack nodded in agreement with Joe's description.

Frank wrote down a few more clues. Under *WHAT* he wrote, *boa constrictor, six feet long, green.* Then under *WHERE* he wrote, *disappeared from glass tank backstage.* "When did you last see him in his tank? Do you remember the time?" Frank asked.

"Little Jim must've seen him last," Jack said. "I had to go onstage first."

Little Jim just kept shaking his head. "Uh . . . I don't remember exactly when," he said. "I saw him before the show started. Maybe ten minutes before. That would have been at around seven twenty, I guess. He was right here, in this tank. I put the red sheet over him before the show started."

Frank scribbled down what Little Jim said. Then he wrote his final question: *WHY?* Frank and Joe's dad, Fenton Hardy, was a detective too. That was

36

how the boys had learned to solve mysteries. Their dad always talked to them about "motive." Motive was a reason someone had for committing a crime. Why would anyone want to take Bubba?

"Can you think of any reason why someone would take Bubba?" Frank asked.

Jumpin' Jack looked under an old table, then under the pumpkin carriage from *Cinderella*. He took a flashlight from his belt and shined it into the bottom of every cage, making sure Bubba wasn't there. "Some kid wanted a pet," Jumpin' Jack grumbled. "That's my guess."

"Or it was those protesters," Little Jim added. "Maybe they did it to make a point. Or maybe it was someone else. A boa constrictor is worth a lot of money."

Joe leaned in, looking at his brother's list. "Or maybe someone is playing a prank on the school. That's possible too."

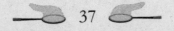

Frank wrote down all the motives in his book, then looked back at the six *W*s. The only suspects they had were the protesters, and there was no way to prove they'd even been inside when Bubba had been taken.

"Did you see anything else? Anything strange before or after the show? Anything at all?" Frank asked.

Jumpin' Jack shook his head. "Bubba was right there," he said, pointing to the tank.

Little Jim scratched the back of his head. "Umm . . . there was one strange thing," he said nervously. "I don't want to get anyone into trouble, though."

"What is it?" Joe asked.

Jim cleaned his glasses on his shirt. Then he took a deep breath. "I saw a girl backstage not too long before the show started. At first I thought she was part of the crew, but she looked out of place. She looked like she was sneaking around."

Frank couldn't help but smile. It was a lead—they had their first real clue. His dad sometimes called clues "leads" because they lead you to answers. "What did she look like? Even if she didn't take Bubba, she might have seen something."

Little Jim shook his head. "I'm not sure. It was so dark, and I was busy. The show was about to start. She seemed to be about your age."

Joe leaned in, looking at his brother's notebook. Frank wrote, *girl, age 8 or 9*, under *WHO*. "You can't think of anything else?" Joe asked. It was good to have a lead, but they didn't have much of a description.

"That's it," Little Jim said. Then he turned back to Jumpin' Jack and helped him search the rest of the stage. "Here, Bubba-ubba-ubba. . . .

Come out, come out, wherever you are," he called to the snake.

Frank and Joe went back into the auditorium, where Cissy, Phil, and Chet were. A few other kids who had helped with the show were there, along with Principal Green. They all looked upset.

"We need to find this girl," Frank said to Joe, looking down at the notebook. "Maybe she saw something. She could know where Bubba is."

But as Joe looked around at his friends, he was

nervous. Cissy was talking about losing the ticket money. The Bayport Elementary Activities Fund had been supposed to use it to help clean up the marina this summer. Phil felt bad that they'd all spent so much time on the show and someone had ruined it. Joe was glad they had a clue, but all they knew was the girl's age. They didn't even know what she looked like.

"You're right," Joe said to his brother. "We need to find her. But how?"

5

An Unusual Suspect

Frank and Joe walked into the school's main lobby, past crowds of parents and kids who were still talking about the missing boa constrictor. A few children were crying. One little boy made his dad hold him up in case the snake was somewhere on the floor.

"What about safety?" one dad asked Principal Green. "There's a snake on the loose somewhere in this school. How are our kids going to come back here on Monday?"

"We're hoping to find the snake within the next few hours. We don't think it escaped," Principal Green said. "We think it was stolen."

As some of the parents talked to Principal Green, Frank and Joe looked around the lobby. There were dozens of girls. Some of the girls went to their school and some of them didn't. Some of them had brown hair and other girls had blond hair. Some were tall and others were short. It was impossible to know which one was the girl Little Jim had seen backstage before the show.

"How are we ever going to find her?" Frank asked. "She could be anyone."

Joe weaved through the crowd, toward the front entrance. He pushed the doors open and walked down the sidewalk. Frank followed close behind. "There was a girl our age who was holding signs with the protesters," Joe said. "We should talk to her. It's a good place to start."

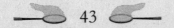

The news van was still outside. The reporter with the giant blond hair was talking into her microphone. The cameras were on. "The search for the missing boa constrictor is still going tonight at Bayport Elementary School," she said. "The *Crazy Critters* show has been postponed until tomorrow night, if they can find Bubba. Meanwhile you'll see behind me that about ten protesters are still here. They want Jumpin' Jack and Little Jim to free the animals."

Frank and Joe walked past the van toward the group on the sidewalk. Two people—and older woman and a girl about Frank's age—held up signs that said GIVE THOMAS THE HAWK SPACE TO FLY! and LET KIPP SPREAD HIS WINGS! As Frank and Joe got closer, they noticed a redheaded girl with freckles standing in front. It looked like she was with her mom.

"Can we ask you some questions?" Frank said as they reached the group. The red-haired woman

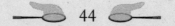

44

lowered her sign. Beside her there was a man wearing a shirt that said WORLD PEACE. His long gray hair was tied back in a ponytail.

"What can we help you with?" the man said.

"We're trying to figure out what happened to Bubba the snake," Joe started. "We know you don't agree with Jumpin' Jack and Little Jim. Do you know anything about what happened?"

"What are you trying to say?" the man said. He crossed his arms over his chest. "Do you think we had something to do with that?"

Frank took a deep breath. "We're trying to get as much information as possible. Little Jim saw a young girl backstage before the show," he explained to the man. "Is it possible you went inside at some point? Did you see anything?"

The red-haired woman grabbed her daughter. "We were out here the whole time!" she said. "We never went inside for even one minute. We don't agree with Jumpin' Jack and Little Jim, but we wouldn't steal their snake."

Frank looked at the redheaded girl. "You never went inside tonight?"

"Not even once," she said, shaking her head. "My mom wouldn't let me see the show."

Frank pulled out his notebook and turned to the page where he'd written *WHO*. He crossed out the word "protesters" from the list beneath it. Joe was leaning over, watching him. "What are you doing?" Joe whispered. "How can we be sure what they're saying is true? You're sure they were outside all night?"

Frank turned around and pointed at the news van. "Look," he said. "The reporter has been standing there, right across the street. The protesters have been on camera the whole time. If they're lying, we'll be able to tell from the news footage."

"But they probably wouldn't lie," Joe said. "Not knowing they'd get caught."

"Exactly," Frank said. He turned back toward the crowd outside the school's front entrance. If this girl was holding signs outside all night, then they were back at the beginning of their search. He was happy they could at least cross off these suspects, but now they had no real clues.

"We should start questioning people to see if they saw anything unusual. We can ask if they saw a girl backstage before the show," Frank said. "Let's split up. Meet me just outside the front doors in ten minutes."

Frank and Joe pushed into the crowd. In a few minutes Frank was surrounded by people. Everyone was talking about what had happened. Most families had decided to leave, hoping that they could come back tomorrow. Frank found a family who'd been sitting close to the stage. They thought they'd seen a shadowy figure in the wings, but they weren't sure. After talking to them for a while, Frank decided it had been just one of the stage crew.

Another third grader said he'd seen a man "acting weird," but when Frank talked to the boy more, it sounded like the man might've just been lost. It didn't seem like anyone else had seen anything odd. Then Frank heard his brother call out from inside the crowd. "Frank! I got something! Over here!"

Joe was standing near the entrance, talking to two eighth graders. Frank had seen them at the local arcade, Fun World, before. They were twins, and they were hard to miss. Both were tall and thin, with curly black hair and green eyes. They were always wearing matching outfits. "This is Lenny and Leo," Joe said. "They saw the girl Little Jim mentioned."

"We went to get a drink from the water fountain a minute or two before the show started. The hallway was completely empty—" Lenny said.

"And that was when we saw her," Leo added, finishing Lenny's sentence. "She was trying to get backstage. We asked her what she was doing, and that was when she ran inside. She—"

"—didn't even answer us," Lenny continued. "She was younger than us, and she had long brown hair and a blue backpack."

Leo frowned. "I thought she had blond hair. But she definitely had the blue backpack on. She was wearing neon green sneakers too."

"Definitely neon green sneakers," Lenny said.

Frank opened his notebook. Under *WHO* he wrote down, *girl with blue backpack and neon green sneakers*. He didn't bother writing down the girl's hair color. He and Joe had worked on enough mysteries to know that witnesses sometimes remembered different things. What mattered was what they agreed on.

"Do you remember anything else?" Joe asked. "Anything unusual about her?"

"That's it," Lenny said. "She went inside really quickly. We didn't get a great look."

"Nothing else," Leo agreed.

Joe and Frank thanked the twins and walked away. "Neon green sneakers," Joe repeated. "I feel like I saw someone wearing those today."

Frank scanned the front of the school and the parking lot, looking for anyone who fit the girl's description. Kids followed their parents to their cars. A group of teenagers sat at the edge of the parking lot. No one had a blue backpack or green sneakers. "I remember seeing them too," he said. "But who wore them? Who was it?"

Joe took the notebook from Frank's hand and looked at the description again. He thought back to the afternoon, when they'd been moving the scenery onto the stage. "That's it!" he cried, suddenly remembering. "It was Cissy. Cissy was wearing neon green sneakers today."

He pushed through the crowd, searching for their friend. He spotted her at the edge of the parking lot. Sure enough, she was wearing neon green high-top sneakers. She looked scared. Her face was pale and she kept glancing over her shoulder, checking to see if anyone was watching her. "She's even carrying a blue backpack," Joe said.

"Cissy!" Frank called out. "We need to talk to you!"

As soon as Cissy heard his voice, she froze. She turned around, a shocked look on her face when she spotted Frank and Joe. Then she started walking even faster, toward the back of the school. Frank and Joe ran after her.

"Cissy, wait up!" Joe yelled.

But within seconds she started to run, disappearing around the side of the building.

6

Free Mickey!

Frank and Joe ran after their friend, turning behind the school building, where everything was dark. Cissy was running toward the school playground. She didn't look back, even when they called her name again.

"Cissy, we just want to talk to you!" Frank said. "Please, wait!"

Finally Cissy slowed down. When she turned around, her eyes were full of tears. "I'm so sorry. I didn't know what to do!" she cried. "I had to help him." She sat down on the seesaw, letting the end hit the ground. Then she put her face in her hands.

"What do you mean?" Joe asked. "Who?"

He'd never seen Cissy so upset. She was the pitcher for their baseball team, the Bandits. She'd gotten the nickname "Speedy" for how fast she could run around the bases. She threw the ball better than any boy they knew, and she was always a good sport, even when their team lost. Frank and Joe had never seen her cry.

Cissy took her backpack off and put it in her lap. Then she unzipped it, showing them what was inside. They could just see the white mouse in the bottom of the bag. Cissy reached in and petted its fur. "It's okay, Mickey," she said softly.

"A mouse?" Frank asked. "Where did you get him?"

"I saw him right before the show tonight," Cissy said. "He was supposed to be part of Bubba's meal tomorrow. But he was so cute and sweet. I kept looking at him in his cage. . . . I couldn't let him get eaten by a snake!" She picked him up and hugged him close to her. Then she petted his head.

"So you were going to take him home with you?" Frank asked. "To save him?"

"Yeah," Cissy replied. "But then Bubba turned up missing, and I was afraid I'd get in trouble too. I didn't have anything to do with that! I have no idea what happened to him!"

Frank took out his notebook and flipped to a clean page. "We should start from the beginning. When did you take the mouse?"

Cissy tilted her head, like she was thinking about it. "It must've been just a minute or two before the show started, because I didn't want anyone to see me. I remember Jumpin' Jack was already onstage. Bubba was still in his tank."

"Did you notice anything strange? Was there

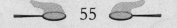

55

anyone else there?" Joe asked. He hoped Cissy could give them more clues. If she hadn't taken Bubba, maybe she'd seen the person who had.

Cissy looked down at the mouse, petting his head again. She waited a moment before saying anything. "Now that you mention it, that red sheet was off the tank. It was lying right beside it. There was a purple-and-blue-striped sack sitting there, like someone had just dropped it. I didn't think it was strange at the time . . ."

Frank wrote everything Cissy said down in his notebook, and listing the purple-and-blue-striped sack. "That is strange," he said. "You must've walked in right as someone was trying to take Bubba."

"Maybe you surprised them," Joe said. "They had time to take off the sheet, but they had to run away before putting it back on."

Cissy nodded. "Now that you say that, it did kind of look that way. And I heard someone run into the dressing room. I just couldn't see them."

"Do you remember anything else?" Frank asked. "Anything at all?"

Cissy shook her head. "I don't," she said. "Please don't tell anyone I took the mouse. Please. I can't let him be snake food!"

Frank and Joe looked at each other. They knew it was wrong to lie. If anyone asked them about the

mouse, they'd have to tell the truth. But they knew Jumpin' Jack was way more worried about Bubba now than anything else. No one had even noticed that the mouse was missing.

"We're just trying to find Bubba," Frank said. "Don't worry, Cissy. I don't think anyone even knows Mickey is gone."

"Come on," Joe said, offering Cissy his hand. "We'll walk you back to the school."

Cissy tucked the mouse back into her bag and zipped it closed. She held the bag carefully as she took Joe's hand, walking with them back toward the parking lot.

Polly's Tasty Treats

There has to be something we missed," Joe said. All the lights were on backstage. The auditorium was almost empty except for Joe and Frank. Jumpin' Jack and Little Jim had gone back to their hotel, and Principal Green was still outside, talking to the last of the parents. Phil was locking up the dressing room behind the stage.

Joe pulled one of the curtains aside, but there was just a broom and mop. Frank walked down the rows of cages, looking at the animals, most of which were asleep for the night. Nothing seemed unusual.

Frank pointed to the door that led into the hallway. "Cissy came in that door, like the twins said. Bubba and the mice were over here," he said, pointing to the other side of the stage.

"Which means she walked behind the back curtain. Whoever took Bubba probably heard her coming and stopped what they were doing," Joe said. "They dropped the sheet. Then, afterward, they probably took Bubba in that bag—it's not here anymore."

Frank looked around the tank again but didn't see anything odd. Joe checked every corner. He checked under the giant pumpkin carriage and behind some props, but there was nothing there either. Had they missed more clues? Where had the person hidden?

"Maybe we should talk to Cissy again," Joe

said, looking around. Frank was checking the cages, which were stacked on top of one another. Kipp the owl had his wings folded around him. Thomas the hawk's cage was covered with a black sheet. Frank kneeled down, staring into one of the bottom cages.

"Look at this," Frank said, pointing inside. There was a tiny gray monkey sitting in the center

of the cage. A sign that said POLLY was on the front of it. "Polly's eating something!"

Joe watched the little monkey. She held a wrapped candy in her hands. She kept turning it over, trying to get the paper off. "Look at the wrapper," Joe said. "It has blue and purple stripes on it."

"Exactly!" Frank said. "Just like the bag Cissy saw."

Joe crawled behind the cage, looking around on the floor. "There's another candy back here," he said. "Look—it's wrapped in the same paper."

He opened it up and stared at the chocolate candy inside. "What do you think it means?" Frank asked. "The candies must've come from the bag Cissy saw. They have to be connected. Whoever took Bubba must've been hiding behind Polly's cage when Cissy came inside."

As they were talking, Phil walked out of the dressing room and locked the door behind him. He pushed aside the curtain and noticed Joe and Frank kneeling on the ground. "What are you guys doing?" he asked. Then he saw the candy in Frank's hand. "How'd you get those candies? They're my dad's favorites!"

"You've seen these before?" Joe asked.

Phil smiled. "Yeah, they're from Artie's. It's a famous candy store near the marina. My dad always goes there for those chocolates. They sell them in a giant bag."

"What does the bag look like?" Frank asked.

Phil held up his hands to show it was a few feet tall. "It's striped, like the candies. Blue and purple. About this tall."

"Do you remember anyone eating these chocolates before the show?" Joe asked.

Phil shook his head. Frank and Joe wanted to ask him more questions, but just then Mr. Hardy appeared at the back of the auditorium. "Boys!" he called out. "I've been looking all over for you. It's almost nine o' clock. Time to go home."

"But, Dad," Frank said, "we're trying to figure out what happened to Bubba the boa constrictor. Whoever took him had a bag from a candy store near the marina. They left behind a few candies. These are our biggest clues!"

Mr. Hardy walked down the aisle, then climbed onto the stage. He looked at the wrapper and candy Frank was holding. "Good work finding that," he said. "But we have to put this on hold, at least for tonight. Your mom is waiting in the car."

"Will you take us to Artie's tomorrow morning, then? Whoever took Bubba bought the candies there. We have to retrace his steps," Joe said.

"I'll take you first thing," Mr. Hardy said. "Now come on. Let's go home."

Frank and Joe followed their dad off the stage, and Phil was close behind. Mr. Hardy plucked the candy from Frank's hand, then took a bite. "That's one delicious clue," he said, and laughed.

"I know," Frank said as he tucked the wrapper into his pocket. "Save some for us!"

8

A Wise Disguise

This is it, Dad!" Joe cried, banging on the car window. He pointed to the store across the street with a blue-and-purple-striped awning. ARTIE'S was written on the front. Mr. Hardy turned, pulling into the parking lot.

As soon as Mr. Hardy turned off the car, Joe and Frank jumped out. In the front window there were three bags just like the one Phil had described. They were sitting up, stuffed with the chocolate candies. Frank pushed inside, Joe and Mr. Hardy following close behind him.

The whole store smelled like chocolate. There were giant lollipops of every size and color. The shelf behind the counter had glass jars filled with gumballs, rock candy, and caramels wrapped in shiny blue foil. "I'm suddenly very hungry," Frank said, eyeing the chocolate-covered pretzels beneath the counter.

"Whoever took Bubba must've had a real sweet tooth," Mr. Hardy said.

Joe walked right up to the counter, where a bald man was putting pink candies into a big glass jar. "Excuse me, but we were hoping you could help us," Joe said. "We think someone who came in here knows about a case we're trying to solve."

Behind Joe, Mr. Hardy held up his badge

to show the cashier. "Do you remember seeing anything strange? Did anyone unusual come in this week?"

The man put the candies aside and scratched his head. His name tag read DWIGHT. "What do you mean by 'unusual'?" he asked.

Frank leaned forward. "Someone who had one of your Artie's bags stole a snake," he said. "It sounds crazy, but it's true."

Dwight's eyes widened. "A real, live snake?"

Joe nodded. "It belonged to Jumpin' Jack, the television host. We're trying to figure out who took the snake."

Dwight shook his head. "That does sound crazy, but now that you mention it . . . there was a man who came in yesterday morning. He had sunglasses on the whole time. I thought that was strange, but I didn't say anything."

Frank glanced sideways at his brother. They'd seen this before in other cases. Sometimes people wore disguises so no one could tell what they looked like. "Do you remember anything else about him?" Frank asked.

Dwight shrugged. "He bought some candy. Then he asked me about that bag in the front window. He wanted to know how many pounds of chocolate it could hold."

"Or just how much it could hold," Mr. Hardy said. "If he used it to take the snake, he probably wanted to make sure Bubba wouldn't be too heavy for it."

"Did he buy the bag?" Joe asked.

"Oh yeah, and everything in it. I remember he had a hat, and he was acting a bit odd," Dwight said. "Give me one second . . ."

He disappeared into the back of the store, then came out a few minutes later holding a laptop computer. He typed a few things in, then pulled up a video. "I bought this security system a few years back, after some teenagers stole a bunch of candy out of the loose bins," he explained. "Here's that guy I was talking about. He came in right around noon yesterday."

Dwight turned the screen around and hit play. The video showed the man at the register, buying the giant bag of chocolates. He had a hat and sunglasses on. "Look what's on his hat," Frank said, pointing to the screen. "It's a snake."

Joe leaned in to get a closer look. Sure enough, there was a tiny snake painted on the front of the man's baseball cap. The camera was too high to show the man's face. He was wearing a black T-shirt, but Joe couldn't tell if he was twenty or fifty.

"Is there any way to get a better look?" Frank asked. "We can't see his face."

Dwight zoomed in, but the picture just got blurry. "I'm sorry. That's the best I can do."

"Do you remember anything else? What kind of car did he drive? Did he have brown or blond hair?" Mr. Hardy asked.

"Was he young or old?" Joe asked.

"Not too young, but not too old," Dwight

said. "It was a busy day yesterday. That's about all I remember. I'm sorry this video didn't help you more."

Then Dwight went back to the glass jar and scooped more pink candy into it until it was full. Frank and Joe followed their dad outside. "We have a suspect," Frank said, getting into the car. "But we don't know how old he is or what he looks like."

"That hat is our only clue," Joe said. He crossed his arms over his chest, feeling more stumped than ever. They were so close, but so far away. What would that guy want with a giant snake?

"Maybe he wanted the snake as a pet," Frank said.

"Maybe," Mr. Hardy agreed as he started the car. "But it's impossible to know. You'll have to keep searching for clues."

Frank looked at the clock in the front of the car. The show was supposed to go on at seven thirty that night, and there was still no sign of Bubba. If they didn't figure out what happened, the school would

lose all the money they raised. All their hard work would be for nothing.

They had to find their suspect soon . . . before it was too late.

9

A Sweet Clue

When Mr. Hardy dropped Frank and Joe off at the school a few hours before the show, Jumpin' Jack and Principal Green were already there. Little Jim loaded some cages onto a cart and started wheeling them off the stage. Inside a bird screeched.

"You promised me you would find Bubba, and you didn't," Jumpin' Jack said. He grabbed a small cage from the ground and put it on Little Jim's cart. "One of your students must've stolen him. What else could have happened?"

Principal Green shook her head. "I'm not sure, but we'll find out. Please don't leave. What about the show tonight?"

Jumpin' Jack stomped around the stage, grabbing a few bags of turtle food and owl pellets. "What about it? I don't perform for thieves!"

Little Jim pushed the cart out a back exit. He kept his head down. His cheeks were red, like he was embarrassed that Jumpin' Jack was yelling so much. "The van should be packed up in twenty minutes," he said. Then he closed the door behind him.

Principal Green put her face in her hands. "What am I going to tell everyone?"

"Not my problem!" Jumpin' Jack said before disappearing into the back dressing room.

Frank and Joe walked up to the stage. Principal

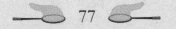

Green sat down on the stairs and let out a deep breath. "What are we supposed to do? Hundreds of people are coming tonight to see Jumpin' Jack. If we cancel the show, we'll lose all the money we raised."

"It was a man who took Bubba," Frank said. "We know that. He was wearing a hat with a snake on it. Does that sound familiar? Did you see anyone yesterday who fits that description?"

Principal Green shook her head. "I didn't see a single person like that."

"We're close to solving this," Joe said. "We just need a few more clues."

"I hope you find them," Principal Green said. She looked at the clock in the back of the auditorium. "Because I'm going to have to tell everyone within the next hour or so. I can't have people arriving for the show."

Frank grabbed his brother's arm and led him onto the stage. "We should question Jumpin' Jack one last time," he said. "He must know something. If a Bayport student didn't take the snake, then Jumpin' Jack might be able to tell us a motive. Why would that man want Bubba?"

The boys snuck backstage, past the last of the cages. Trixie the monkey snickered as they walked by. When they reached the dressing room, Jumpin' Jack was in his massage chair. Frank knocked on the door to wake him up.

"What isssss iiiit noooow?" Jumpin' Jack asked, his voice rumbling. "I'm trying to relax for just one minuuuuuute."

"We're trying to figure out who took Bubba," Joe said. "But we wanted to ask you a few more questions."

Jumpin' Jack turned the chair off and sat up. "Okay, fine. What?"

Frank looked at his brother and frowned. As much as he loved Jumpin' Jack's show, he was starting to think Jack wasn't that nice a person. He was mean to everyone, even his biggest fans. "We think whoever took Bubba went into a candy store yesterday near the marina," Frank said. "He bought a giant sack of candy, then used a cloth bag to take Bubba. It was blue and purple."

"Did you see anyone carrying a bag like that?" Joe asked.

Jumpin' Jack rolled his eyes. "No, I didn't see anyone like that. And if all you know about the guy is that he liked candy, that's a serious problem. I'm probably the only person in the world who *doesn't* like sweets!"

"We're hoping the candy clues mean something," Frank said.

But Jumpin' Jack just stood and grabbed his green jacket from the chair. He put it on and pushed past Frank and Joe and went out the door. "This is useless," he said. "I'm going to bring the last of our stuff outside. It's starting to seem like Bubba is gone for good."

Then he left, not saying anything else. Frank was about to run after Jumpin' Jack, but Joe stopped him. "Did you hear that?" Joe asked, his eyes wide.

"What?"

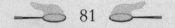

"He doesn't like candy!" Joe said, practically yelling. Then he looked at Frank like he was supposed to know what that meant.

"So what?" Frank said.

"So . . . everything!" Joe cried. He ran over to the table in the dressing room, pointing to all the bowls of candy. There were gummy bears and chocolate bonbons. Lemon drops sat in a big pile. "If Jumpin' Jack doesn't like candy, remember what Phil told us?"

Frank smiled, finally understanding. "He was the man at Artie's," he said. "The one with the hat. He must have worn it to cover his crazy hair."

"Come on," Joe said, running toward the door. "We need to find him!"

10

The Show Must Go On

Frank and Joe ran across the parking lot to where the *Crazy Critters* van was. Jumpin' Jack was standing at the back door, looking at all the animals. "That's right, Trixie," he said, sticking his finger into the monkey's cage. "We're heading out soon. Don't worry."

"Wait!" Frank called. "Where's Little Jim? We need to talk to him."

"He ran off somewhere," Jack said. "He's always

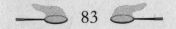

running off just when I need him to do something. Why?"

"Does Little Jim have a baseball hat with a snake on it?" Joe asked.

Jumpin' Jack didn't answer. Instead he went around to the passenger side of the van, reached through the window, and pulled out a blue hat. A tiny green snake was curled up on the front. "You mean this?"

"That's the one!" Frank cried. "Little Jim stole Bubba. We're sure of it."

"You've got to be kidding me," Jack said, and laughed. "Why would Little Jim steal Bubba? He has a snake of his own, and he sure doesn't need the money."

"We don't know why," Frank said. "But we're trying to find out. Which way did he go?"

Jumpin' Jack pointed toward the other side of the school, near where the gym was. "He said he had a few more things to do inside. He went that way."

Frank and Joe took off toward the side doors of the school. When they got to the gym, it was empty. Only Mr. Miles, the janitor, was there sweeping the floor. "Did you see Little Jim, the guy from the show last night?" Frank asked. "He has crazy white hair."

Mr. Miles rested his chin on the end of the broom. "Sure did," he said. "He went toward the art wing. Seemed like he was in a hurry."

Joe thanked Mr. Miles and followed his brother down the hall, past rows of lockers. There were giant paintings hanging on the walls. The art wing was filled with clay vases and wire sculptures, some hanging from above. "Do you hear that?" Joe whispered. He grabbed Frank's shirt so he would stop walking. "Listen."

Now that it was quiet, Frank could hear footsteps somewhere up ahead. It sounded like someone was running away from them. They crept along the wall and peered around the corner. Little Jim was walking quickly toward the end of the hall. He looked around before stopping at a broken locker.

"What is he doing?" Frank whispered. They inched back, making sure he couldn't see them.

Little Jim leaned down and opened the locker, then pulled out a bag. It was the same blue-and-purple-striped bag they'd seen earlier at Artie's. Only, this one had something in it. Little Jim could barely carry it, it was so heavy. He grabbed it with both hands and started walking away.

"It's Bubba!" Joe whispered.

Frank knew what they had to do. He jumped out from behind the corner. "Little Jim, we know you have Bubba!" he called out.

Little Jim froze, his white hair sticking up

in every direction. He looked at the door at the end of the hall, which was still twenty feet away. He couldn't run fast and carry Bubba at the same time. Frank and Joe had finally caught their suspect.

"Please," Little Jim said, holding the bag tight. His cheeks were bright red. "I can explain . . ."

He pulled the snake from the bag and let it curl around his arm. "Jack was going to give Bubba to a zoo in New York!" he said, petting the snake on the head. "As soon as we were done with our book tour, he was going to ship him off. I raised this snake since he was just an egg. He's like a friend. I couldn't let that happen."

Frank and Joe looked at the snake, the infamous Bubba. It was cool to see him up close. He was huge, with black spots all over his body. He glided up Little Jim's arm and around his shoulder, as if he were giving him a hug.

"Why didn't you just say something?" Joe asked. "Why did you steal Bubba?"

"I tried to tell Jack to keep him, I did. But he never listens to me!" Jim said. "And right before the show, Jack said he might ship him off today. I was scared I wouldn't have another chance to

save him. I brought Bubba to this locker to hide him during the show. Then I was going to bring him back home in my suitcase."

"What about the show?" Frank said. "You could have told us where he was. They were going

to cancel it, and our school would've lost all the money they raised."

"I didn't want Jack to get mad at me," Little Jim said. "I'm sorry, I am. I just didn't know what to do. Once everyone was looking for Bubba, I didn't feel like I could tell people I had him."

Little Jim held the snake against his chest. He kept petting Bubba's head. "What should we do?" Joe asked his brother.

"We have to bring him back," Frank said. "Even if Jack gives him to the zoo. We don't have a choice."

Little Jim's eyes filled with tears. "I know," he agreed. "I'm just sad to say good-bye to him."

Frank and Joe walked back toward the auditorium, knowing they had finally solved the case. They knew who had taken Bubba and why. But Frank still didn't feel great about it. Bubba would live the rest of his life far away from here. He'd never go on any more crazy adventures with Jack and Jim. Jim would never see him again.

"We should go," Joe said. "The show has to start soon."

That night Frank and Joe sat in the front row of the auditorium with Principal Green, watching the *Crazy Critters* show again. The whole room was packed with people. Kids laughed when Jack brought out Trixie the monkey. Kipp the owl did a few extra tricks. But the highlight of the show was the big reveal. This time when Jim pulled the red sheet off Bubba's tank, the snake was actually there.

"You two saved the day," Principal Green said, clapping as Jack and Jim took their final bows. "Without you we never would've found out what happened to Bubba, we would've had to cancel the show, and everyone in Bayport would be asking for their ticket money back."

Frank and Joe stood up with the rest of the crowd. They clapped as Jack stepped forward with Bubba wrapped around his shoulders. Frank tried to smile, but it felt fake. "If we saved the day," he whispered, "why don't I feel better? I hate the idea of Bubba in a zoo."

Jack stood onstage, looking out at the cheering crowd. Some people were snapping pictures with their cell phones. Other people raised their arms and cheered. Everyone seemed so happy.

"As some of you know," Jack said, "Bubba was . . . *misplaced* last night. We've got our Crazy Critter back, but tomorrow he'll leave the show and join the animals at the New York zoo." Jim stood beside Jumpin' Jack, his face sad. He kept wiping his eyes with the back of his hand.

"As much as we'll miss him, I decided to give him to this zoo because he needs more room to grow," Jumpin' Jack said. "There he'll have a whole huge pen to himself to do what snakes do best . . . slither and slide around."

A few first graders beside the stage laughed, repeating Jack's words. He sometimes said "slither and slide" on the show, making the *S*s long to be funny. As Jumpin' Jack kept talking, Little Jim

looked better. He started to smile a bit, and he even laughed.

"We want Bubba to be the best boa constrictor he can be, and that means giving him his space. He'll leave for now, but Little Jim and I will visit him as much as possible. Right, Jim?"

Little Jim smiled. "I'm going to be visiting the zoo once a month to talk about reptiles and all the crazy adventures Jack and I have been on. I'll make sure to tell you how our good friend is doing." This time his whole face lit up.

"So Little Jim will get to see Bubba again!" Frank said, smiling.

"Yeah," Joe said. "And hopefully Jim will keep us posted on Bubba during *Crazy Critters*."

The audience clapped and cheered as Jumpin' Jack and Little Jim raised their arms in the air, then bowed their final bow. The curtains closed, but the crowd was still cheering. Frank and Joe clapped so much, their hands hurt. Not only had it been a great show, but it looked like Jumpin' Jack, Little Jim, and Bubba the boa were all going to be okay.

SECRET FILES CASE #17: SOLVED!

Nancy Drew and the Clue Crew®

Test your detective skills with more Clue Crew cases!

Visit NancyDrew.com for the inside scoop!

From Aladdin · KIDS.SimonandSchuster.com

Join Zeus and his friends as they set off on the adventure of a lifetime.

Now Available:

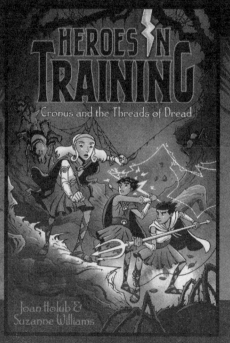

#1 Zeus and the Thunderbolt of Doom

#2 Poseidon and the Sea of Fury

#3 Hades and the Helm of Darkness

#4 Hyperion and the Great Balls of Fire

#5 Typhon and the Winds of Destruction

#6 Apollo and the Battle of the Birds

#7 Ares and the Spear of Fear

SHARK SCHOOL

Dive into the world of Harry Hammer in this fin-tastic chapter book series!

Discover shark facts, downloadable activities, and more at sharkschoolbooks.com.

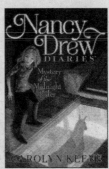

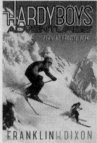